I Love You All Day Long

Special Thanks to my family: Pat, David, and Danny for your love
and support; to my mother, Bobette, a champion of dreams

To my friends: I am deeply grateful to my talented editor,
Margaret Anastas, and to my dear friend Q. L. Pearce,
and of course to Priscilla Burris for sharing the journey.
—F. R.

For my Craig, Janelle, Laura, Paul,
and especially Ruben & Lily Garcia,
and Omer & Harriet Burris,
who continue to love us all day long!—P. B.

I Love You All Day Long
Text copyright © 2003 by Francesca Rusackas • Illustrations copyright © 2003 by Priscilla Burris

Library of Congress Cataloging-in-Publication Data
Rusackas, Francesca.
I love you all day long / by Francesca Rusackas ; illustrations by Priscilla Burris.
p.   cm.
Summary: When a little pig worries about being apart from his mother when he goes off to school, she reassures him.
ISBN 0-06-050276-2 — ISBN 0-06-050277-0 (lib. bdg.) — ISBN 0-06-050278-9 (pbk.)
[1. Mother and child—Fiction.   2. First day of school—Fiction.   3. Schools—Fiction.   4. Pigs—Fiction.]
I. Burris, Priscilla, ill.   II. Title. • PZ7.R892 II   2003   2002001177 • [E]—dc21
Typography by Stephanie Bart-Horvath
❖

I Love You All Day Long

by Francesca Rusackas
illustrated by Priscilla Burris

HarperCollinsPublishers

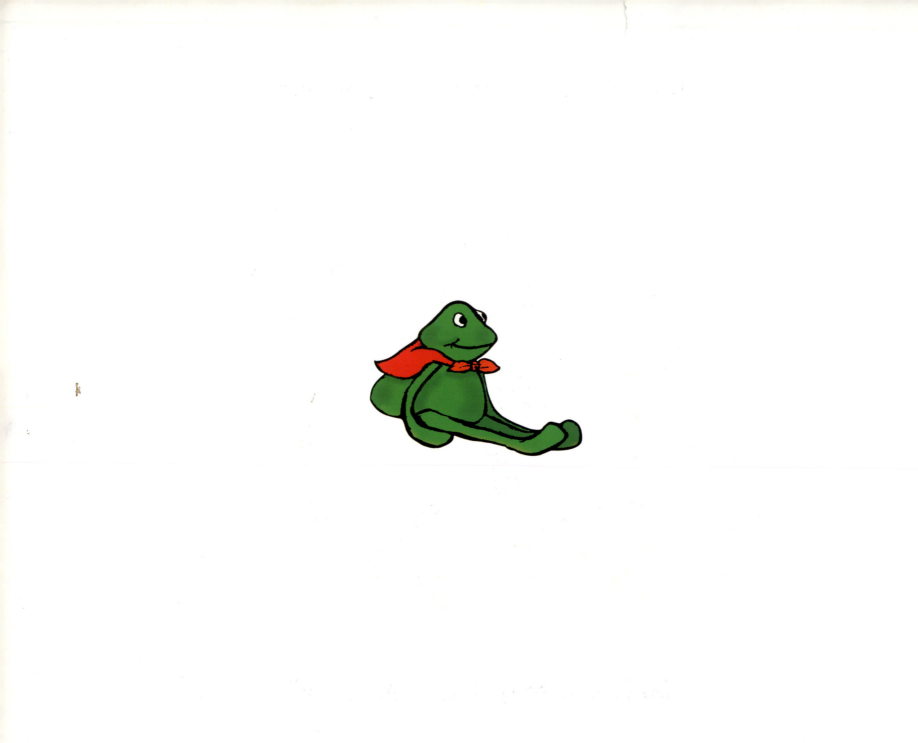

Owen had an important question:

"Do I have to go today, Mommy?"

"Yes, you do have to go today," said Owen's mommy.

"But, Mommy," whispered Owen,

"you won't be with me!"

"That's right, Owen," said his mommy.
"But you should always remember this:

I love you when I'm with you

and I love you when we're apart."

"That means you love me all day long!" said Owen.
"You're so right, sweet one!" said Owen's mommy.

"I love you all day long."

"I love you when you make a new friend."

"I love you when you share your favorite purple crayon

or when you make a mistake."

"I love you when you trip over your shoelaces

or when you sing 'Itsy Bitsy Spider' all by yourself.

I love you all day long."

"I love you when you march to a *clang-clickity-clang*

and I love you when you let a burp sneak out."

"I love you when you're last in line

or when someone takes your toy.
I love you all day long."

"I love you when you accidentally make a mess

or when you can't wait for the bathroom."

"I love you when your juice spills

and when your crackers get soggy. I love you all day long."

"I love you when you wait for your turn

or when you climb too high."

"I love you when you have to call for help.

I love you when you figure things out for yourself."

"I love you when you follow directions

or when it's your turn to feed the fish."

"I love you when you fly into my arms
and when you hug me as tightly as you can."

"I love you all day long!"